Zheng He

Zheng He (say: *Jung Her*) was a **navigator** who lived in China around 600 years ago. He was selected by the Chinese emperor to command an **expedition** of sailing ships to far-off lands. The emperor's plan was to demonstrate to other rulers the power and glory of the Chinese Empire.

In the year 1405, the fleet set sail from Nanjing with 317 vessels carrying more than 27 000 people, including sailors, soldiers and **scribes**. The fleet was comprised of 40 warships, as well as 47 transport ships carrying horses, 48 supply ships packed with food and 20 tankers filled with fresh water.

a brass depiction of the Chinese explorer Zheng He

The largest and grandest ships in Zheng He's fleet were 62 treasure ships painted with fierce dragons to scare away the spirits of the sea. The treasure ships were loaded with Chinese goods, such as silks, cotton and spices, to trade with other nations and to impress foreign rulers.

Zheng He's fleet faced many potential challenges. Shipwreck was a constant danger, especially along the rocky coastlines, and the ships' crews also faced the threat of losing contact with one another in poor weather conditions.

Additionally, bands of pirates roaming the Strait of Malacca near Sumatra (Indonesia) preyed on trading ships. It was Zheng He's responsibility to keep his huge fleet intact.

Zheng He's enormous fleet contained more than 300 ships.

Several important Chinese inventions supported Zheng He in his mission. Detailed maps were drawn on long charts made of paper, which the Chinese had invented centuries earlier.

Zheng He navigated with the help of a magnetic compass.

To aid navigation, they had also invented a **magnetic compass** that helped determine a ship's position far from land. Communication between ships was made possible by drums, gongs and carrier pigeons.

The fleet's first port of call was Champa (South Vietnam), where Zheng He presented the king with magnificent gifts to show that he came in peace. In turn, the king led Zheng He on a tour of his rice fields and temples.

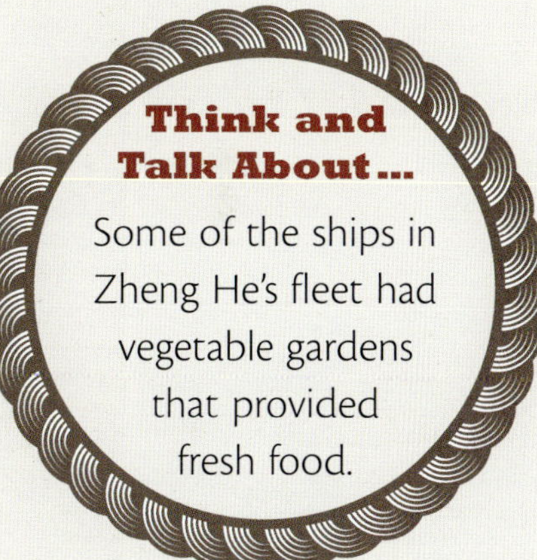

Think and Talk About ...

Some of the ships in Zheng He's fleet had vegetable gardens that provided fresh food.

After visiting several other ports where goods were exchanged, the ships crossed the **treacherous** Indian Ocean to reach the west coast of India. For several months, the treasure fleet remained in the ancient port of Calicut until trading was completed, and the ships were loaded with precious Indian spices, including cinnamon, ginger and pepper.

Passing through the Straits of Malacca on the return voyage, the fleet's warships engaged in a fierce battle with pirates. Many pirate ships were destroyed by the well-trained soldiers who aimed showers of flaming arrows at their sails.

As the ships crossed the South China Sea, they were caught in a violent storm. Towering walls of water, driven by powerful winds, threatened to sweep the ships towards the rocky coast. Scribes on board the ships recorded how Zheng He called to the goddess of Chinese sailors for help, and the seas immediately grew calm.

Finally, after a journey of almost two years, Zheng He brought his fleet safely home. The voyage had been a great success, and the emperor was delighted.

To this day, the voyage of the enormous treasure fleet is believed to be the largest ocean expedition in world history.

Zheng He's Return Journey from China to India

INTREPID Journeys

Jill McDougall

Contents

Aboriginal and Torres Strait Islander people should be aware that this text contains names and images of people who are deceased.

Courage and Daring

An intrepid journey is one that is dangerous and which often requires great courage and daring.

Throughout history, humans have undertaken **perilous** journeys for many reasons. Some are driven by curiosity and a need to explore new places. Others are adventurers seeking fame and fortune, or are **missionaries** seeking to spread Christianity to foreign lands. During times of hardship, such as war, people often undertake intrepid journeys in search of safety.

No matter what the nature of the journey is, it is always accomplished with elements of determination and **fortitude**, as well as a powerful will to survive.

Over time, some people who have undertaken intrepid journeys have become well known for their feats.

Captain James Cook was a famous explorer who undertook many intrepid journeys, including the first European expedition to Australia.

Today, many statues of Zheng He can be found in China.

Christopher Columbus

In 1492, Italian explorer Christopher Columbus was planning a daring sea voyage. He hoped to find a way to reach the Indies from the coast of Spain. The Indies, known as Asia today, were thought to be rich with spices, gold and silk, but these goods could only be transported to Europe via a dangerous route across mountains and deserts.

a portrait of Christopher Columbus

For Columbus, the solution was to find a sea route to the Indies, thus guaranteeing both fortune and fame for himself. In the 1400s, Europeans were ignorant about the wider world. Until that time, people had believed the Earth was flat, and they had no understanding that there were large **continents** on the globe, including those now called North America and South America.

While Columbus believed the Earth was round, he thought it was much smaller than its true size. He decided he could reach the Indies in no more than a fortnight by sailing west across the Atlantic Ocean.

On 6 September 1492, Columbus set sail from Palos in Spain with three small wooden ships, the *Pinta*, the *Niña* and the *Santa Maria*. The ships carried stores of food, such as cheese, honey and raisins, as well as wooden barrels of wine and water.

From the beginning of the voyage, many of the sailors were afraid of what lay ahead. The Atlantic Ocean had never before been crossed by a European ship, and there were fearful beliefs about boiling seas and horrifying sea monsters. After 30 days at sea (much longer than they had expected), the crewmen became restless and threatened to turn the ships back to Spain.

Christopher Columbus' fleet contained three ships.

A few days later, land was sighted and, on 12 October, Columbus set foot on a small island that he named San Salvador. He was convinced he had reached the Indies but, in fact, he had arrived in the Caribbean Sea, thousands of kilometres from Asia.

Columbus spent two weeks sailing around the Caribbean Sea, searching in vain for the gold he hoped to take back to Spain. When he traded goods with the local **indigenous** people, they offered him colourful parrots and bows and arrows, but they had very little gold.

Christopher Columbus lands on San Salvador.

As the fleet prepared to return home, the *Santa Maria* was wrecked on rocks and the ship had to be abandoned. The two other ships returned safely to Spain, and Columbus, who was still sure he had been to the Indies, was given a hero's welcome.

Although Columbus failed to find a sea route to Asia, his daring journey opened up an era of discovery and exploration that was to last for centuries.

Christopher Columbus's First Voyage

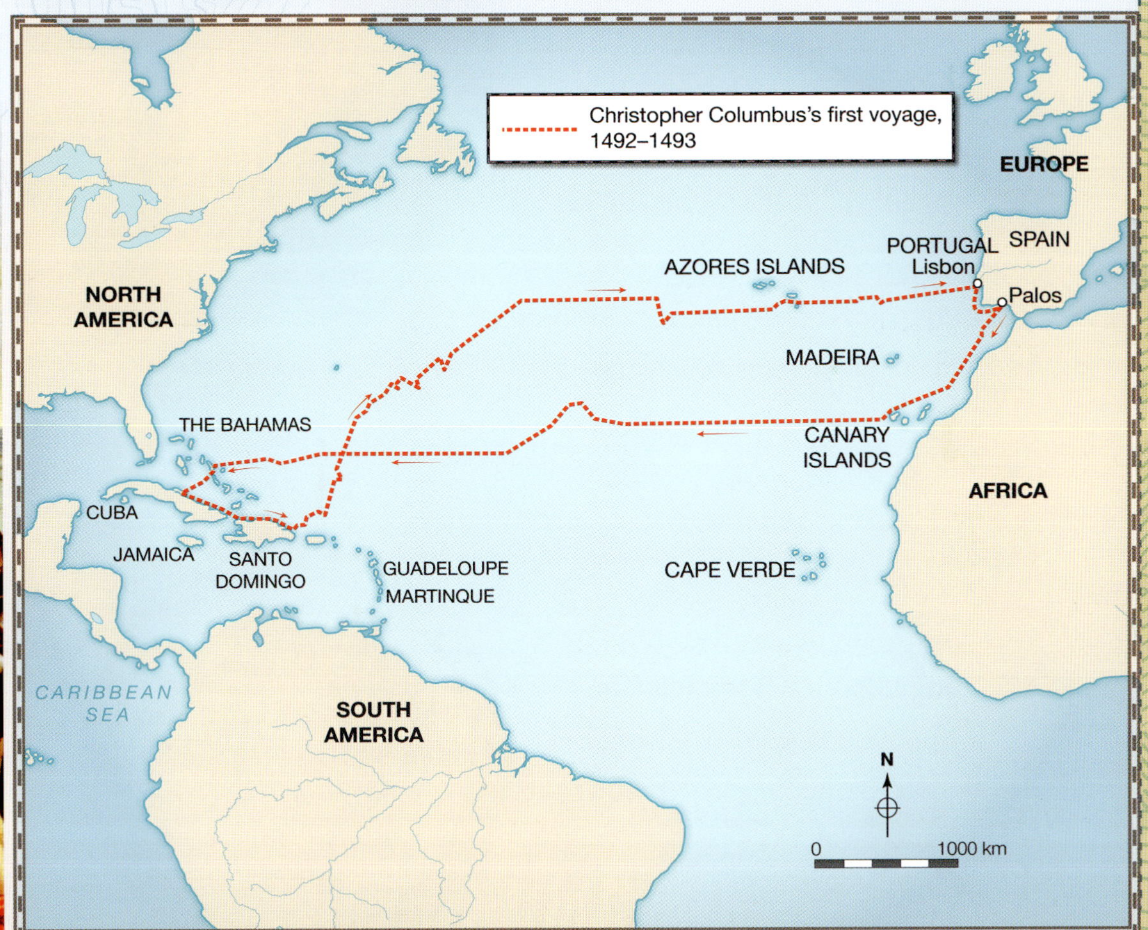

Ernest Shackleton

In 1914, British explorer Ernest Shackleton sailed towards Antarctica from South Georgia Island on his wooden ship, *Endurance*. He and his men planned to walk across the vast ice continent, via the South Pole.

As *Endurance* sailed into the Weddell Sea close to Antarctica, floating ice gathered around the ship and hardened like cement. Before long, the ship was trapped.

For nine months, the 28 members of the expedition remained on *Endurance*, waiting for the ice to break up. However, after a storm, heavy ice began to grind against the ship and, bit by bit, the ship's strong timbers buckled and broke. Soon, the ship was sinking.

The crew swiftly unloaded the ship's stores and set up tents on a nearby **ice floe**. This cold, wet campsite, which they called "Patience Camp", remained their home for many months.

a portrait of Ernest Shackleton taken in around 1909

Think and Talk About ...

At Patience Camp, the men burned seal blubber to create warmth, and ate many meals of seal stew.

When the ice floe began to break up, the men launched three lifeboats into the water. All day and all night, they sailed and rowed through stormy seas, hoping to reach land. By the sixth day, the men were desperate with lack of sleep and food.

The crew, which included several dogs, made a makeshift camp after their ship was trapped.

Finally, the men found land around 500 kilometres from Patience Camp. But it was little more than a frozen rock in the bleak ocean, known as Elephant Island. As the wind howled around them, they turned their lifeboats upside down on the beach and sheltered underneath.

Shackleton knew he would have to urgently get help or his men would not survive. Over 1200 kilometres away lay a **whaling station** on South Georgia Island. Shackleton would try to reach it with five men and the strongest boat, the *James Caird*. The remaining crew stayed on Elephant Island.

The men sheltered under their lifeboats on Elephant Island.

Ernest Shackleton and five members of his crew departed Elephant Island to find help.

Early one morning, Shackleton and his men embarked on their desperate journey. From the beginning, waves swamped their boat, drenching them in freezing water. After a few days, their fresh water was gone and the men could barely speak for thirst.

After 16 long days, Shackleton spotted the black cliffs of South Georgia Island. As they stumbled onto dry land, he and his men were exhausted. However, their ordeal was not yet over. To reach the whaling station they had to cross **glaciers** and high mountain ridges – a journey that no one had ever managed.

Shackleton and two of his strongest men set off and, before long, they became trapped on an icy ridge. Above them was sheer rock and before them lay thick, swirling fog that shrouded the landscape.

The men were faced with a terrible choice – they could freeze to death or leap off the cliff into the unknown. One by one, they leapt into the swirling fog and fortunately landed safely on a snow bank.

Thirty-six hours after setting off, the three weary men reached the whaling station. The three men on the other side of South Georgia Island were quickly rescued and, three months later, the group on Elephant Island was brought to safety.

Ernest Shackleton's incredible journey is considered to be one of the greatest survival stories ever told.

5 December 1914
Endurance departs South Georgia Island.

1915

18 January 1915
Endurance is trapped in ice.

27 October 1915
Endurance is crushed.

30 October 1915
The crew starts the march.

21 November 1915
Endurance sinks.

21 December 1915
Patience Camp is established.

1916

9 April 1916
Boats are launched for Elephant Island.

15 April 1916
Shackleton lands on Elephant Island.

24 April 1916
Shackleton departs on the *James Caird*.

10 May 1916
Shackleton arrives at South Georgia Island.

19-20 May 1916
Shackleton and two men cross the mountains and reach Stromness whaling station.

30 August 1916
Shackleton reaches Elephant Island and rescues the rest of the crew.

Ernest Shackleton's Antarctic Voyage

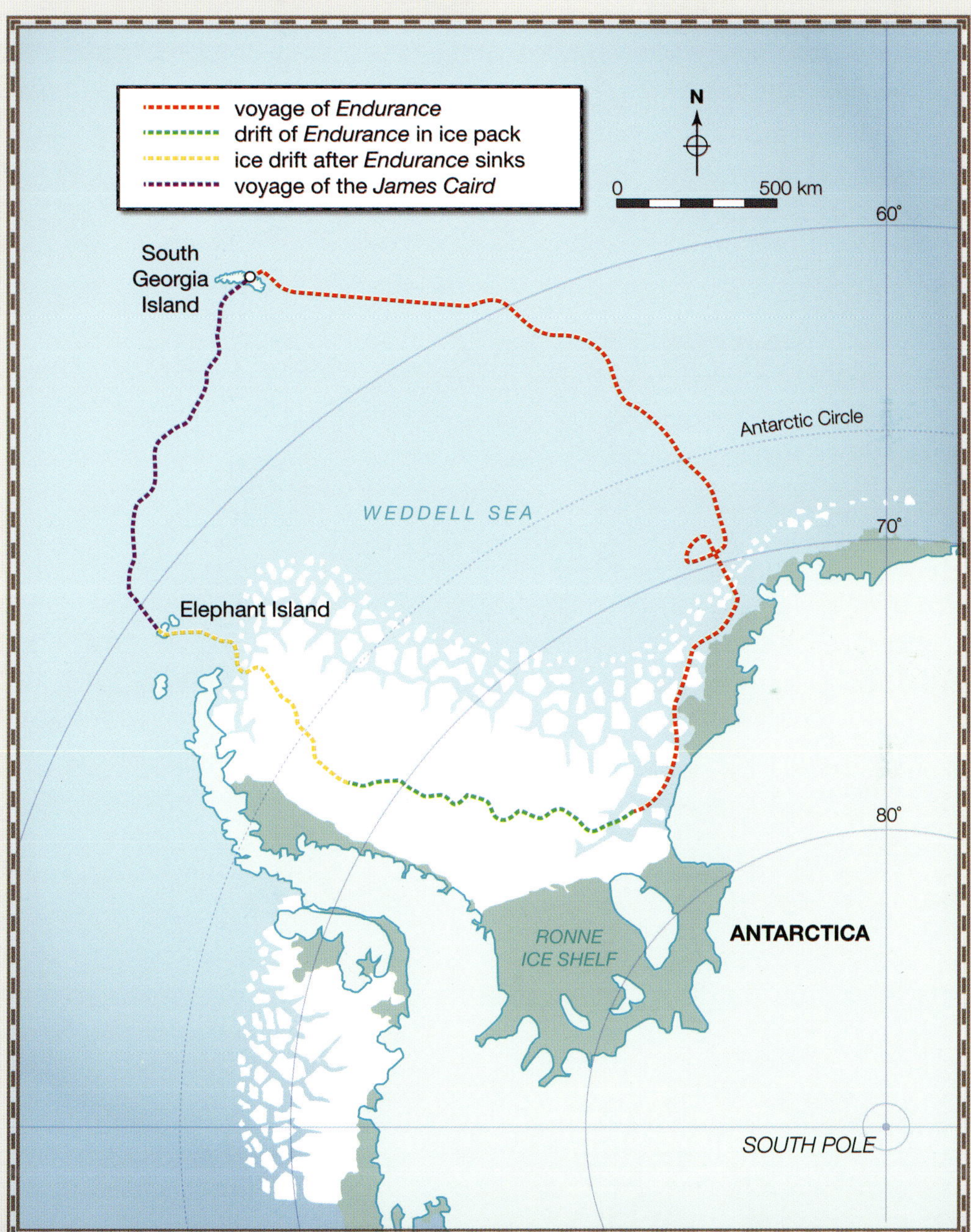

Amelia Earhart

In May 1932, an American pilot named Amelia Earhart was ready to make a historical journey. She wanted to become the first woman to fly alone across the Atlantic Ocean. At that time, small aeroplanes were fragile and unreliable, and this made long solo flights risky. Earhart's daring plan was to fly a small **monoplane** from Canada to Europe.

Amelia Earhart in 1927

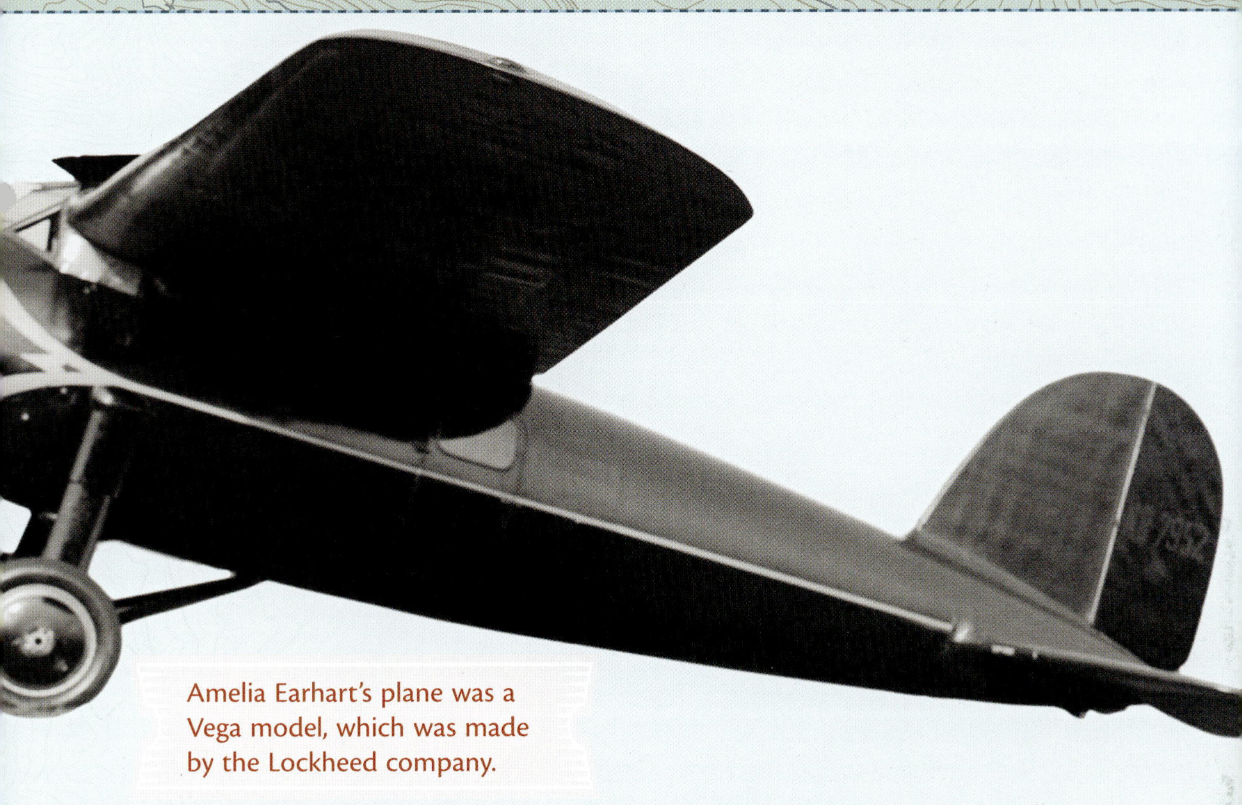

Amelia Earhart's plane was a Vega model, which was made by the Lockheed company.

The weather was calm when Earhart took off from Newfoundland, an island in the Atlantic Ocean off the east coast of Canada. However, a few hours later, she flew into fog. Ice began to form on the wings of her small plane, threatening to send it into a deadly spin. Earhart quickly adjusted the plane's **altitude**, flying lower over the ocean to melt the ice in the warmer air.

Not long after, Earhart ran into a severe thunderstorm. Strong winds buffeted the tiny plane, and the altimeter, which measured the plane's height, was damaged. Despite this setback, Earhart remained calm and flew on steadily through the long, lonely night.

As the bright light of morning appeared, the smell of petrol fumes began to fill the **cockpit**. The reserve fuel tank had developed a leak, so now Earhart faced the danger of running out of fuel. The bitter fumes irritated her eyes and the dazzling reflection of the sunlight made it almost impossible to see.

Nearing the limits of her **endurance**, Earhart searched for land. She noticed a fishing boat, then several more, until finally the coastline of Ireland came into view. Earhart followed a railway track, hoping it would lead to an airfield, but all she could see were farms.

Although she could not find an airfield, Earhart decided to land, so she brought her plane down bumpily in a soggy field, scattering a herd of cattle. She had landed in Culmore, Northern Ireland.

Amelia Earhart was given a hero's welcome when she landed.

As Earhart came to a stop, she checked the cockpit clock. The crossing had taken almost fifteen hours, which meant she had broken the record for the fastest crossing over the Atlantic Ocean.

Once Amelia Earhart arrived in London, she was surrounded by photographers and newspaper reporters. News of her amazing flight soon spread around the world, and her fame skyrocketed.

When she sailed home to the USA, every vessel in New York harbour sounded its whistle, and army planes flew low overhead. Later, Earhart was awarded one of her nation's highest honours, the Distinguished Flying Cross.

In the years to come, Amelia Earhart undertook many other daring flights across the world. Her spirit of adventure inspired many others, both men and women, to follow their dreams.

Amelia Earhart's Flight Across the Atlantic

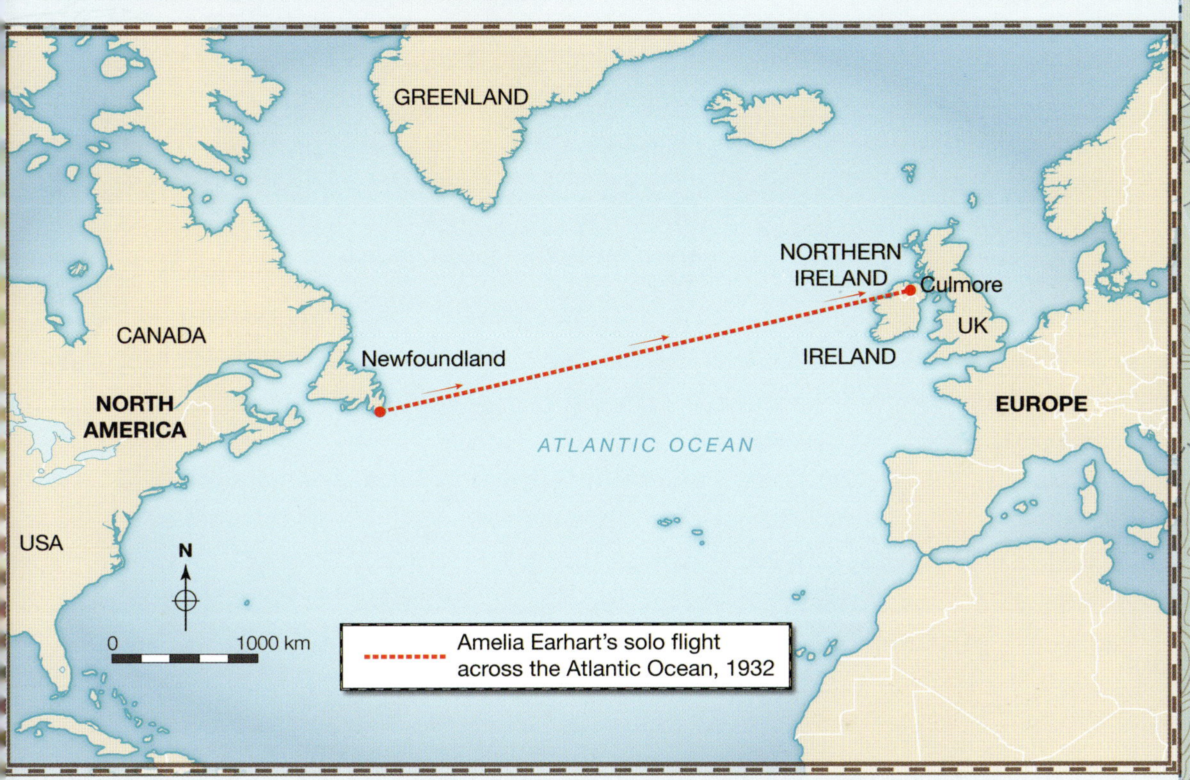

Amelia Earhart was awarded the Distinguished Flying Cross by President Herbert Hoover.

Think and Talk About ...

In 1937, Amelia Earhart disappeared while flying her plane around the world. A fragment of it was not found until 1991.

Molly Craig

In 1931, 14-year-old Molly Craig lived in Jigalong, a small Aboriginal community in the north of Western Australia. One day, a police officer took Molly, her younger sister Daisy and her cousin Gracie away. In those days, there was a policy in Australia to separate many Indigenous children from their parents, so the three girls were taken to a **mission school** north of Perth. They would be educated at this school and trained as domestic servants.

Molly Craig (left) and her daughter Doris Pilkington stand near the rabbit-proof fence in 2002.

The school, known as the Moore River Settlement, was more than 1000 kilometres from Jigalong. Conditions were harsh. The children slept in large, cold dormitories with iron bars on the windows and were forbidden to speak their native language.

The three Jigalong girls were scared and homesick, so Molly, who was a natural leader, decided that they should escape and return home.

Molly knew that Jigalong was not far from the rabbit-proof fence. This fence runs over 2000 kilometres from the north of Western Australia to the south. It is comprised of three different sections and was built to keep rabbits and other animals out of farming areas.

Molly decided that if the girls walked eastwards from Moore River, they would eventually reach the fence, which they could then follow north to Jigalong.

The girls' first challenge was to cross the fast-flowing Moore River. Molly found a tall gum tree that hung over the water, and the girls climbed along its trunk, swinging themselves across to the other side.

The rabbit-proof fence was built between 1901 and 1907.

Day after day, Molly led Daisy and Gracie in the direction of the rabbit-proof fence. They crossed wheat fields, climbed sand dunes and trudged across scrubby plains. At night, they slept in dry gullies and under bushes.

All the while, Molly was terrified they would be caught. She knew they would be taken back to Moore River, where they would have their heads shaved as punishment and then be locked up for days. She was grateful when rain fell and covered their tracks.

After a month of hard walking, the girls finally reached the fence and turned north for home. However, they still had another 800 kilometres to travel.

In the more settled areas, the girls were given food and clothes by kindly farmers' wives, but when they reached the desert areas, they depended on their hunting skills to survive. From a young age, the girls had been taught how to find food, such as wild bananas, and how to catch rabbits and young birds.

After passing the town of Meekatharra, Gracie, who was feeling footsore and weary, decided the trip was too tough to continue. At a railway **siding**, she met some people who told her that her mother was at Wiluna, so she boarded a train to the settlement. She was later captured and returned to Moore River Settlement.

After nine long weeks, Molly and Daisy walked into Jigalong and were reunited with their grateful relatives.

The young girls' amazing journey ranks as one of the most remarkable feats of endurance and courage in Australian history.

Molly Craig's Journey Across Western Australia

Against Incredible Odds

The intrepid journeys of Zheng He, Christopher Columbus, Ernest Shackleton, Amelia Earhart and Molly Craig tell a tale of daring and determination. They demonstrate the power of the human spirit to overcome great challenges and survive against incredible odds.

Zheng He

Christopher Columbus

Ernest Shackleton

Amelia Earhart

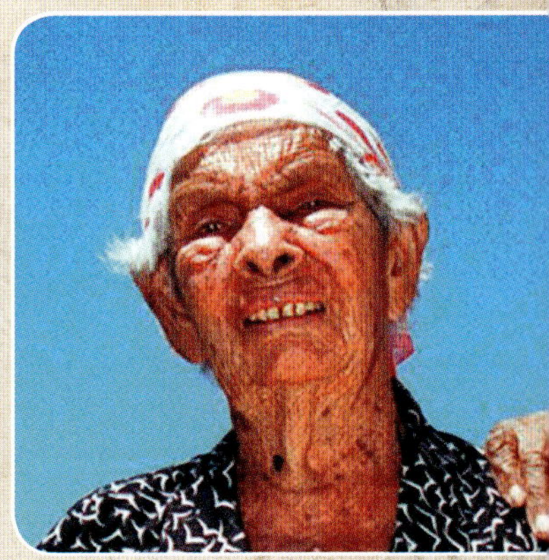

Molly Craig

MAKE A MAGNETIC COMPASS

GOAL

To make a compass that functions in the same way as the ones used to guide Zheng He's treasure fleet

MATERIALS

You will need:

- a sewing needle
- a flat piece of cork
- a pie dish
- a magnet.

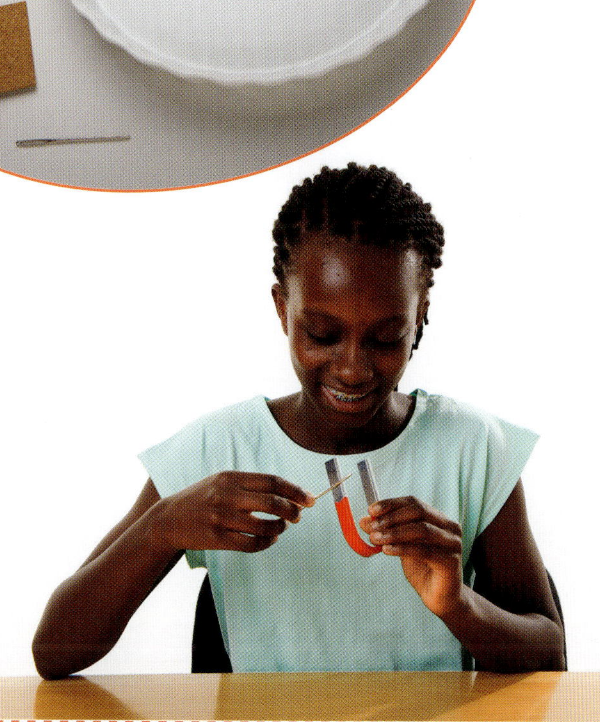

STEPS

1. Stroke the magnet along the needle 15–20 times.

2. Fill the pie dish with water and place the cork on it.

3. Centre the magnetic needle on the floating cork.

4. Very slowly, the needle will swing into a north-south orientation.

Glossary

altitude (*noun*) the height of an object

cockpit (*noun*) the space in a plane for the pilot

continents (*noun*) large land masses usually surrounded by water

endurance (*noun*) the ability to withstand a difficult situation

expedition (*noun*) an organised journey with a special purpose

fortitude (*noun*) mental strength in facing difficulty

glaciers (*noun*) slow-moving rivers of ice

ice floe (*noun*) a flat piece of ice that floats on the sea

indigenous (*adjective*) the original inhabitants of a certain place

magnetic compass (*noun*) an instrument that uses a steel bar to show direction

mission school (*noun*) a school run by missionaries

missionaries (*noun*) people sent to another country or area to do religious work

monoplane (*noun*) an aeroplane with one pair of wings

navigator (*noun*) an officer who directs the course of a ship

perilous (*adjective*) full of danger or risk

scribes (*noun*) people who keep records of events

siding (*noun*) a low-speed section of a railway track

treacherous (*adjective*) something that is very dangerous

whaling station (*noun*) a place where whales are processed (cut up) to be sold

Index